THE KING'S DAUGHTER

Ann Musico

AmErica House
Baltimore

First printing

ISBN: 1-58851-577-X

PUBLISHED BY AMERICA HOUSE BOOK PUBLISHERS

www.publishamerica.com

Baltimore

Printed in the United States of America

DEDICATION PAGE

To my Elizabeth, who has taught me what it means
to be a true princess and to all the other King's
daughters who will realize their rightful place in
His kingdom.

"Mommy, may I use your white high heels so I can pretend I'm a princess?" Eight-year-old Elizabeth loved imagining she was a beautiful princess, dressed in the finest clothes, wearing a sparkling jewel-covered crown and living in a huge palace! It was one of her favorite pretend games.

"Sure you can, honey," said her Mom. "But first come here. I want to ask you a question."

Elizabeth walked over, but she was very impatient to get those shoes so she could start playing. "Elizabeth, I've noticed lately that this has become your favorite game. Can you tell me why you think being a princess would be so wonderful?" asked Mom.

Elizabeth didn't hesitate for even one second. "Well, princesses are beautiful. They have the prettiest clothes in the world. They get to wear a crown covered with diamonds and rubies. Everyone is excited to see them and hear what they say, and people do whatever they tell them to because their dad is the king."

"Wow!" exclaimed Mom. "You've really thought carefully about all this, haven't you?" Elizabeth nodded her head. "Well, before you go off to play, I have one more question for you. What would you say if I told you that you actually are a real, live princess?"

Elizabeth, for once, was speechless! If that were really true, it would just be the best news she could ever imagine. "Mom, what do you mean? How could it be true? We don't live in a palace, I don't have a crown and Daddy is a teacher, not a king." The more Elizabeth tried to figure it out, the more confused she became.

"Do you remember when you were five and you asked Jesus to come and live in your heart?" asked Mom.

"Sure I do," said Elizabeth.

"Well, I don't think you realize everything you got that wonderful day. When Jesus came into your heart, you became a child of God, His daughter, right?"

"Right. He's my Daddy in heaven and Daddy is my father here on earth."

"Exactly. Your earthly dad is a teacher, but your heavenly Dad is the King of the Universe." For a minute all Elizabeth could do was stare.

Her Mom continued, "Well, think very carefully about that for a minute. It makes sense that if you are a daughter of your heavenly Daddy and He is the King, then you really, truly are a princess! Fancy clothes, crowns and palaces don't make you a princess. Your relationship to the King makes you a princess."

This was almost more than Elizabeth could believe. As she let what her Mom said sink in, it began to make perfect sense. All of a sudden her eyes began to sparkle and she cried in delight, "I see it! I get it! I am a real, live princess in God's kingdom right now!"

"Exactly! But there's more to being a princess than just wearing a crown and having people bow to you and do whatever you tell them to."

"Like what?" asked Elizabeth dreamily, still picturing herself sitting on a huge throne, telling people what to do.

"Well, wherever a princess goes, she represents her father, the king, and his kingdom. People decide whether they think he's a good king or not by how she behaves."

Whoa! That made Elizabeth stop and think seriously for a minute. "Do you mean that if I feel cranky and act mean to someone, that makes people think God isn't good?"

"Well, not exactly. But it may make them wonder if you really love your Dad the King since you don't behave the way He tells you to in His book, the Bible. It may even make them wonder if you really are His daughter."

Elizabeth was very confused. "Mom, I don't think I understand."

"Sweetie, once you asked Jesus into your heart you became God's daughter forever. That never changes, no matter what. Even on your crabbiest day, He still loves you more than all the oceans in the world. He sees your heart. He knows you love Him and always want to please Him, even though sometimes you mess up. As long as you admit your mistakes to Him and you are truly sorry, He forgives you and forgets it ever happened," explained Mom.

"So, then why does what I do matter so much if God loves me no matter what?" asked Elizabeth, puzzled.

"The difference is that other people don't see what's in your heart like your Daddy God can. They only see how you behave and hear what you say. If someone knows who your Dad is, and they see you lie or use bad language or make fun of someone, they might think, 'Wow, I guess it's OK to do those things since His own daughter does them.' Then you would cause them to stumble, which means they might sin because of what they saw you do." Elizabeth just sat there quietly, not moving a muscle.

Mom continued, "The Bible tells us if we really love God, we will do what He says. One reason is so that others can see that what God tells us to do is always best. When they see that you want to obey Him and do whatever makes Him happy, then they'll be curious to get to know Him, too."

Elizabeth was very quiet for a few minutes thinking about everything Mom just explained. Finally, her eyes lit up and she exclaimed, "Yes! I get it now. When I do what God says, it makes other people see I love Him and trust Him because He's such a good Dad. Then they will want to get to know Him better because I love Him so much."

Mom was just nodding her head and smiling. "Exactly! Let me go and get you my shoes so you can play princess now."

"That's OK, Mom," said Elizabeth with a big smile. "I don't really need them now. I think I already have everything I need to be a princess!"

"I know you do!" said Mom, giving Elizabeth a great, big hug.

2

"Mom, I think it's so cool that I really am a princess, a real, live daughter of the King!" Elizabeth bounced downstairs for breakfast with a happy smile.

"I do have a question, though," she said thoughtfully.

"And what is that?" asked her Mom as she toasted a bagel for Elizabeth's breakfast.

"Well, since I don't have to wear a crown or live in a palace to be a princess in God's kingdom, exactly what can I do to show I am being a good princess so people will love my Heavenly Father as much as I do?"

"Hmm. That's a wonderful question, Elizabeth. I am happy to see that you are really taking this seriously." Mom stood quietly thinking about Elizabeth's question for a minute. Finally she said, "You are growing up so quickly. You're already finishing third grade. Your classroom is upstairs on the second floor. Your report card has real number grades, not just 'O's' and 'S's'. You've even had to do a big typed report just like your older brothers do."

Elizabeth was quietly nibbling away at her bagel and listening to Mom with a serious look on her face.

Mom continued, "Each day will bring different situations for you to handle. Some will be with friends, some here at home; others will have to do with what you want to do. Every time you have to make a choice about how to act or what to say or do, you have a golden opportunity to represent your Dad, the King."

Elizabeth took a sip of orange juice and said, "I know that, Mom. I'm asking if you can tell me exactly how to do it."

Mom was quiet for a minute and then she said, "I can't really tell you what to do specifically in every, single choice you'll have to make, because I don't know what decisions you may have to make today. Maybe we can put our heads together and come up with a good way to help you. Let's both think about it and we'll talk more after school today, OK?"

Elizabeth brightened, "OK, Mom."

When Elizabeth got home from school, her first question was, "Well, Mom, did you think of anything that will help me be a good princess?"

Mom sat down next to Elizabeth and said, "Elizabeth do you know what a slogan is?"

Elizabeth looked puzzled. "I'm not sure."

Mom continued, "It's a catchy phrase companies use to help people remember what they're selling. You hear them on commercials all the time."

"Oh, you mean like 'the cheesier macaroni and cheese'?"

"Exactly."

"OK, but how will that help me?" Elizabeth was a little confused.

"Well, I was thinking we could come up with a slogan you could try and remember each time you find yourself having to make a choice," said Mom.

"Like what?" asked Elizabeth.

"I was thinking that since you want to speak and behave in a way that pleases your Heavenly Dad, maybe before you make any choice you could just ask yourself, 'What would a princess choose to do?' Then after you think it over or talk about it with me or Daddy if you need to, you can make a decision that will please God."

Elizabeth was just sitting perfectly still, a serious look on her face.

"Well, what do you think?" asked Mom.

Finally, Elizabeth's face burst into a huge, sunny smile. "I love it, Mom! It'll be easy to remember and it will help me act the way a true princess would."

"Honey, don't feel badly if you forget sometimes while you are trying to make using your slogan a habit. It takes some time and practice to remember to do something new. But if you keep trying, soon it will become automatic," said Mom.

"Thanks, Mom. I can't wait to try out my new slogan and show everyone what a wonderful Dad God is!"

3

"Do you think we could go clothes shopping this weekend? I need some new spring clothes." There are not too many other things Elizabeth loves to do more than shop!

"Have you tried on last year's shorts and t-shirts to see what still fits you?" asked Mom.

"Yes, Mom. A lot of them still fit, but I really wanted to buy a few belly shirts like the ones my friends wear," said Elizabeth.

"Belly shirts? What are those?" asked Mom.

Elizabeth replied, "You know, Mom, what all the models wear in the magazines. They're short shirts that show your belly."

"Oh, I see," said Mom slowly. "I think we have to have a little talk about how princesses dress."

"You mean I have to ask what a princess would choose to wear? I didn't think God cared so much about how I dress!" exclaimed a surprised Elizabeth.

"Your Father God cares about everything you do. Your clothes are actually very important to Him because the way you dress says a lot about what you want people to think about you."

"Oh," said Elizabeth gloomily. "I guess that means belly shirts are out."

"Well, let's talk about a princess's wardrobe and you can decide for yourself if they'd be a good choice. OK?" asked Mom.

"I guess so," said Elizabeth slowly.

"You know it's important to be well-groomed. That means having clean hands and nails, hair that is clean and combed, face washed and teeth brushed. It also means wearing clothes that are clean, no holes or rips and that fit you properly."

Elizabeth was listening carefully so Mom continued.

"God also tells us in His Word that because He loves us so much He wants us to put on certain behavior every day, kind of like 'spirit clothes'."

"Really?" said Elizabeth. "Like what?"

"The first one is compassion. That's a big word that means you feel happy when others are happy and you feel sad when they are sad. That could be like the prettiest dress you could ever imagine."

Elizabeth was beginning to get interested now, "What else?"

"The next one is kindness. That's when you look for ways to do good things for others. That could be a beautiful blouse with a lace collar."

"Cool!" said Elizabeth excitedly.

"Then there is humility. That means putting others ahead of yourself and not being a know-it-all. No one likes a know-it-all, do they?"

Elizabeth shook her head 'no'.

"I guess humility could be a soft, fluffy sweater with fancy flower buttons. Then there is gentleness. Do you know what that one means?"

Elizabeth thought for a minute and then said, "I think it means to treat people as if they could break easily."

"That's a wonderful way to describe gentleness!" Mom was very pleased. "Let's make gentleness a pretty, long flowered skirt. Now there's patience, being able to wait your turn calmly, with a good attitude. What piece of clothing do you think patience could be?"

"I'd make patience be a pair of fancy white sandals with colored beads on them!" squealed Elizabeth.

"There is one last and most important item that pulls the whole outfit together and makes it look perfect. Can you guess what that is?"

Elizabeth thought for a minute. Finally her eyes lit up and she said, "I think it's love because that's the most important thing we can do, love each other! Am I right?"

Mom smiled at her. "Yes, you are exactly right. Now about that belly shirt…"

Elizabeth didn't even let Mom finish. "Mom, I changed my mind about that. I think a princess would make a better choice. Besides, I have all those other beautiful 'spirit clothes' that will make even shorts and a t-shirt look special!"

4

"Elizabeth, you look awfully tired. Didn't you sleep well last night?" asked Mom with concern.

"No, I didn't. I was worrying and tossing and turning all night," said Elizabeth.

"What were you worrying about?"

"I kept thinking about the big tests I have coming up this week. Then I have tryouts for basketball and I'm afraid I might not do very well. My head is so full of worries it feels like a balloon that's ready to explode!" said Elizabeth with tears in her eyes.

Mom sat next to Elizabeth and put her arm around her. "Honey, I surely can understand that you feel overwhelmed by all these things you have coming up. Have you asked what a princess would choose to do about it?"

Elizabeth shook her head miserably. "No, I didn't. I forgot to."

"What if we talk about it and figure out how Father God would want you to handle this?" asked Mom.

"I think that would help," said Elizabeth wiping her eyes.

"We know that God is the perfect Dad, right?" Elizabeth nodded and Mom continued. "Well, do you think a good father would want his children to be worried, nervous and afraid?"

"No, of course not. When I tell Daddy I'm afraid about something he asks me to tell him about it and after I do, I always feel better," said Elizabeth.

"Right, and Father God tells you to do the same thing. He tells us in the Bible to cast our cares on Him. Do you know what that means?" asked Mom.

"I'm not exactly sure."

"Well, to 'cast' something means to throw it off and 'cares' are all the things worrying, scaring or bothering you. So God is saying to take every single thing that's worrying you, or making you feel nervous or afraid, whether it's big or small, and throw it off onto Him!"

Elizabeth looked puzzled. "But how do I do that?"

"Good question. Just like you tell Daddy about what's upsetting you, you can tell God what is worrying you by praying," explained Mom.

"I've been trying to do that, Mom, but after a little while all of a sudden all the things I told God about pop back into my head again and I'm back where I started, thinking and worrying."

"Hmm. Well, I think I have an idea that might help you. Let's make a worry box!"

"A worry box? What's that?" asked Elizabeth.

"Well, we can take one of your old shoe boxes and cover it with wrapping paper. You can use your little rainbow pad to write each of your worries on. For each worry we can look up a verse in the Bible that tells what God promises to do to help you. Then you can cast it into your worry box. Whenever the worry pops back into your head, you can go and read the promise. This way you get the worry out of your mind and replace it with the promise. Do you think that might help you?"

Elizabeth had been listening very carefully and now she smiled for the first time this morning and said, "I'll get the shoe box, let's make it right away!"

So Elizabeth and Mom found some pretty flowered wrapping paper and covered one of her old shoeboxes. Then they took two pieces of paper from her little rainbow colored pad and wrote on one sheet, ' Doing well on tests' and on the other, 'Basketball tryouts'.

"Well, we have the worries written down, now comes the fun part. Let's find a verse for each that tells how God promises to help," said Mom smiling.

"OK, let's do it!"

Together they looked through Elizabeth's Children's Bible and talked about each problem. Elizabeth had studied and done all her homework, so she did everything she could do to be ready for her tests. She even practiced her dribbling and free throws every chance she had to be ready for tryouts. So she had done all she knew to do. Now she and Mom found two verses to replace the worries. On the sheet about doing well on her tests they wrote: 'I can do whatever I have to because Jesus always helps me' from Philippians 4:13. On the sheet about basketball tryouts they wrote: 'No matter what I do, help me to do it in a way that makes You proud, God' from 1Corinthians 10:31.

"Now all you have to do is 'cast' them into your worry box and trust that God is helping you," said Mom.

Elizabeth dropped them in and put the lid back on. "I feel so much better now, Mom. I think this worry box will really help me to forget my worries and remember what God promises me."

5

"I'm so angry I could just…I could…well, I don't even know what I could do!" sputtered Elizabeth as she dropped her book bag on the floor and sat down.

"What happened?" asked Mom.

"A girl in my class told my best friend Marissa that I said she wasn't my friend anymore and I never said that! Now Marissa is probably mad at me. I'm so angry with that other girl for telling a lie about me. I'm not going to forget this. I won't ever talk to her again!" The words just came gushing out of Elizabeth.

"I can see why you're so angry. That was very unfair. Feeling angry is a normal reaction when someone treats you unfairly or is mean to you. Have you asked how a princess would choose to handle this?" asked Mom.

"No, I guess I was too angry to think about much of anything," said Elizabeth.

"Do you remember where we read in your Bible about the time when Jesus was being arrested and killed for something He didn't do?" Elizabeth nodded. "He was treated worse than anyone else who's ever lived. They told lies about Him, hit Him, spit on Him, made fun of Him and finally they hung Him on a cross. Wouldn't you say that was pretty unfair?" asked Mom.

"Yes it was. It was awful," said Elizabeth seriously.

"Honey, God knew there would be times when you would feel angry. It's part of how people are made. We have many different feelings. We can feel happy, sad, tired, angry, confused, proud, nervous and hurt. Feeling angry is a natural part of being human. But because you are His daughter and He cares so much about you, he tells you that you can feel angry, just get over it quickly and don't hold a grudge."

"What's a grudge, Mom?"

"That just means not to stay angry and keep remembering what that person did to you. Do you remember what Jesus said about the people who did all those awful things to Him while He hung on the cross?"

Elizabeth said, "I think I do! He asked Father God to forgive them."

"Right!" said Mom. "Do you know why it is so important to get over your anger and forgive the person who hurt you?"

"No, why?"

"Well, when you're angry you open a door for the devil to stick his foot into your life. Once he has his foot in the door, he can keep feeding you angry thoughts and before you know it, your joy is gone!"

Elizabeth was listening but she was still having trouble with the idea of forgiving the girl who lied about her. "Mom, if I forgive her, it's like saying what she did was OK. It wasn't and I don't want her to think it was."

"Sweetie, I understand how you feel. When you forgive someone you aren't saying that what they did was OK. You are saying you will let go of your anger about it and let God deal with the person. Forgiving someone takes the job of making the person understand what they did and why it was wrong, off of you, and puts it on God, where it belongs. God will always be fair even though people sometimes aren't. Once you tell God that you forgive that girl, He can start showing her in His own way what she did wrong and you can be full of joy again, instead of angry."

"I think I get it, Mom. I don't think it will be easy, but I trust God to take care of this for me, so I will choose to forgive because I'm His daughter and He tells me to."

"I'm so proud of you, Elizabeth," said Mom smiling. "I know it isn't easy, but it makes me happy to imagine Father God smiling as you just slammed the door in the devil's face! Now, why don't you call Marissa and explain what really happened. I'm sure she knows you two will always be friends."

"Thanks, Mom. I feel much better already and I'll feel even better when I get everything back to normal with Marissa."

****6****

"Mom, some of my friends are going to see the new movie everyone is talking about. I really want to go, too. I don't want to be the only one who doesn't see it," said Elizabeth sadly.

"Honey, we've talked about this movie. First of all it's rated PG-13 and you are almost nine. There are some violent and scary scenes in it and Daddy and I don't feel it's something we want you to see. I can't speak for your friends' parents, but God gave us the responsibility of taking care of you and the answer is no," said Mom firmly.

"Mom, I know shooting and hurting people is wrong. Why can't I just see the movie? I would never do any of those things."

"That isn't exactly the whole point. Let me see if I can explain it to you in a different way. How do you feel if you think about something scary, like a nightmare where someone was chasing you?"

"Well, I actually start to feel scared if I think about it long enough."

"That's because your feelings follow what you think about. If you think about something sad, you could start crying about it all over again. If you think about fun, happy things, you start to feel happy. You think about things that have happened to you, or things you've seen, heard or read about. All those things stay tucked away in your memory and any time you want to, you can remember them. Sometimes they'll pop into your head even when you don't want them to. That's why it is so important to choose carefully what kinds of things you watch on TV, or in a movie, or read in a book or hear on the radio. All those things become part of your memory, whether you want them to or not."

That was a lot for Elizabeth to take in. She just sat there for a few minutes trying to think it all through. Finally, she said, "I think I get it. Your brain is kind of like a computer. Whatever you see and hear you're programming in, the way Chris programmed the math games into our computer for me."

"Exactly right. What a good way to explain it!" said Mom.

"Mom, does God say anything in His Word about how I can think the way a King's daughter should?"

"As a matter of fact, He does! He says we should think about things that are true, good, kind and beautiful. We should think loving thoughts about others and about things that make us want to praise God."

Elizabeth nodded her head, smiling. Mom continued, "The choice is yours. God doesn't force you to think right thoughts. He lets you decide how to program your own memory. If you choose to put junky things in that make you feel sad or scared or confused or angry, you really can't blame anyone but yourself."

"I see what you mean. I have to learn to make good decisions about what I store in my brain because it can pop back up into my memory," said Elizabeth.

Mom was nodding her head and smiling, "Besides, why would anyone want to carry around a head full of junk when God made so many wonderful things to fill our minds with?"

****7****

"I feel so sad for Leslie, Mom, I could just cry!" said Elizabeth.

"Why? Who's Leslie and what's wrong with her?" asked Mom.

"She's a girl in my class. She's always getting in trouble for talking, acting goofy and not doing her work. She's short and can't run very fast, so when we all play tag, she always loses. She gets into fights with some of the other girls because they tease her and won't let her play with them at recess. She was crying today because a couple of girls told her she's weird and stupid." Mom could see that Elizabeth was very upset about this.

"Do you think she's weird?" asked Mom.

Elizabeth didn't answer right away, and when she did it was in a whisper, "I just think she's different."

"Do you think it's bad to be different?" asked Mom.

"I don't know, I just know if you're different sometimes people are mean to you."

"You're right about that. It's never right to treat someone badly just because they're different. After all, God made us all different from each other. Some of us are tall, others are short, some can sing, others can paint, some can run fast, others write poetry, some love sports and others love ballet! Every single one of us is very precious and special to God exactly as we are."

"I know that, Mom, but it would be easier if she'd just act more like everyone else. Then they wouldn't tease her so much," said Elizabeth miserably.

"I understand you hate to see her get her feelings hurt, but having her be just like the rest of the girls isn't the answer. Imagine what it would be like if every single one of the girls in your class all looked exactly alike. Imagine they talked the same way with the same voice, thought the same thoughts, wore the same clothes, were all the same height, were good at the same things, and liked exactly the same things. What do you think that would be like?"

Elizabeth sat there picturing this in her mind, a class full of girls who were all exact copies of each other, like dolls in a store window. After a minute she said, "It would be boring! It would be kind of like being all alone since no one would have a different idea and everyone did everything exactly the same way. It would be like talking to yourself! I don't think I'd like it at all."

"I agree with you. The same way God created all the different, interesting animals and insects in the world, and all the different colors and kinds of flowers, He made each and every one of us a special masterpiece!" said Mom.

"You're right, Mom. Remember the hundreds of cool, different colorful fish we saw at the aquarium last year? If they were all medium-sized, blue fish, it wouldn't have been very interesting to see. But there were little yellow ones, and big red ones, and medium striped ones and huge blue ones. It was so cool!"

Mom nodded, "It sure was."

"I guess since I'm His daughter, God wants me to see others the way He does, right?" asked Elizabeth.

"Right," said Mom. "It's very important to understand that just because someone is different, it doesn't mean they're not as good. It just means God is giving you the chance to learn from someone who sees things in a different way. What do you think you can do to show Leslie that you accept her just the way she is?"

"Well," said Elizabeth thoughtfully, "I could sit with her at lunch, and ask her if she wants to play hopscotch or jump rope at recess. I could ask if she needs help with some of her work, too."

"That sounds like a wonderful start. I bet some of the other girls will stop teasing her when they see how you treat her. You know she may act silly and get in trouble because she's upset or worried about something that's going on at home. Maybe someone is sick or in trouble and she doesn't have anyone to talk to about it," said Mom.

"I could just try and be a friend and listen if she wants to talk, too."

"I think that's a great idea and I think Leslie is lucky one of the King's daughters is in her class!" said Mom with a smile.

8

"Is something bothering you, Elizabeth? You've been so quiet and sad the past day or so." Mom was very concerned about Elizabeth, who was usually bubbling with laughter and full of life.

Elizabeth looked down at her feet and then said slowly, "I really messed up, Mom. I lost my temper with a boy in my class and I really hurt his feelings. He kept fooling around and talking to me and I couldn't finish my work. I asked him over and over again to please stop, but he wouldn't. Instead of asking myself what a princess would choose to do next, I finally just lost my patience and yelled at him in front of everyone! He looked so embarrassed. I just feel awful. I really messed up. He probably hates me now."

"Honey, I know how disappointed you are with yourself for losing your temper. It happens to everyone sometimes. It won't do you any good to keep punishing yourself and feeling bad, though," said Mom.

"I'm afraid to even talk to him. He'll probably never speak to me again," said Elizabeth.

"The first thing I think you need to do is to go to your Heavenly Dad and admit your mistake. You see whatever we do to another person, it is just like doing it to God. When one of his children is hurt, He hurts, too, because He loves each of us so much."

"Oh, Mom, now I feel even worse. I didn't only hurt Bobby, I hurt God, too!" Elizabeth was almost in tears.

"Wait! God tells us what to do to make everything right again. First you confess what you did. All that means is you tell God what you did and agree with Him that it was wrong."

"That's easy. I know I was wrong. Should I tell Him right now?" asked Elizabeth.

"Sure. Why not?" asked Mom.

"OK," said Elizabeth, eager to make everything right. "Father, in Jesus' Name I come to You and say

I lost my temper with Bobby. I admit I was wrong and I'm very sorry."

"That was perfect," said Mom. "Now, the next thing is to repent. All that means is to change your mind about what you did and go in a different direction."

"So can I say this? Father, I'm sorry I didn't act the way Your daughter should and I'll do my best not to act that way ever again, but I need You to help me," prayed Elizabeth.

"Exactly! Now you can relax and know that God has forgiven you and He doesn't even remember what you did wrong! Wasn't that easy?"

Elizabeth nodded her head.

"Well, now comes the last part and I guess the hardest part. Do you know the five hardest words to say to someone?" asked Mom.

"No. What are they?"

"They are, 'I'm sorry. I was wrong.' And that's pretty much what you need to say to Bobby."

"I'm afraid he'll run away from me or stay mad," worried Elizabeth.

"He might, I guess, although I really don't think he will. Either way, you still need to apologize in order to make everything right. That's your part. Bobby's part is either to accept your apology or not. Whatever he decides to do, you are still responsible to do the right thing, and then trust God to do the rest," said Mom.

"OK. I'll go and tell him I'm sorry first thing this morning before I even start 'problem of the day'," said Elizabeth.

"I bet you'll be pleasantly surprised by his answer," said Mom.

The first thing Elizabeth said when she walked in the door that afternoon was, "You were right Mom. Bobby forgave me and we're still friends. He was afraid I was mad at him for bothering me when I was trying to work! God's ways are always best!"

9

Elizabeth had been practicing asking 'what would a princess choose to do' every time she had to make a decision.

When her brothers wanted to watch a baseball game and she wanted to watch one of her shows, she had to ask that question and choose what to do.

When Mom was really busy trying to get dinner ready and picking the boys up from baseball practice, she had to ask the question and choose to set the table without being asked.

There were lots of chances every day to practice being a daughter of the King.

"Elizabeth, you've been trying very hard these past few weeks to remember to ask God what choices to make. Is it getting easier to remember?" asked Mom.

"Yes, Mom, it is. Sometimes I still forget at first and remember later on."

"What do you do when that happens?" asked Mom.

"I just ask when I do remember and try and choose the right thing to do anyway," said Elizabeth.

"Good for you! Just keep in mind that you're trying to start a new habit. You know how hard it is to break a bad habit, like biting your nails. It takes a while to change something you've gotten so used to doing. Well, it's also hard to make a new habit part of your life. You can't get upset with yourself when you forget. Just do what you are already doing and go right back and do it when you remember. Pretty soon you will just ask that question without even having to think about it. It will just become your normal way of doing things."

Elizabeth nodded, smiled and said, "It makes me feel better to know God doesn't get mad at me when I forget. It makes Him happy that I am trying to please Him. Being a princess is even better than I ever imagined!"